SADIE and RATZ

SONYA HARTNETT

ILLUSTRATED BY
ANN JAMES

WALKER
BOOKS

For Hannah — who else?
S.H.

For Joan Haycraft
A.J.

This edition first published in Great Britain 2010 by Walker Books Ltd
87 Vauxhall Walk, London SE11 5HJ

4 6 8 10 9 7 5 3

Text © 2008 Sonya Hartnett
Illustrations © 2008 Ann James

The right of Sonya Hartnett and Ann James to be identified as
author and illustrator respectively of this work has been asserted by them in
accordance with the Copyright, Designs and Patents Act 1988

This book has been typeset in Bembo Educational
and Blockhead

Printed and bound in China

British Library Cataloguing in Publication Data:
a catalogue record for this book is available from the British Library

ISBN 978-1-4063-2540-9

www.walker.co.uk

Chapter One

I am Hannah. These are my hands. Their names are Sadie and Ratz.

We live in a house with my mum and dad and my stick insect, Pin. I want a dog, but Mum says I'm too young.

Until I am older, I can only have
a stick insect. "And Sadie and Ratz,
don't forget," says Dad. Sadie and Ratz
aren't animals. "But they behave like
wild beasts," says Dad.

These are things I like:

purple
ladybirds
ponies
soft toys with sad eyes

When I am kind, these are things I do:

tickle Dad's ear
stroke Mum's hair
wobble Grandma's stomach

These are things that Sadie and Ratz like:

crunching

squishing

squeezing

They also like piranhas.

Sadie is the boss. She is the same size as Ratz, but she is meaner.

When Sadie grows up, she wants
to be a dragon. When Ratz grows up,
he wants to be a bigger Ratz.

Ratz does what Sadie tells him to do.
Together, they make a good team.

This is what they do:

crush things up
twist and scrunch
scratch! scratch!
scratch!

When Sadie and Ratz are on the rampage, look out!

There is someone in our house
I forgot to mention.

Baby Boy

I wish he was a dog.

'Boy' by Hannah

Baby Boy is four years old. Four
years is a long time. It seems like
Baby Boy has been around for ever.
Everyone says Baby Boy is a good
boy. But these are things that Baby
Boy does:

goes into my room

changes the TV channel

**uses all the coloured
felt-tips**

15

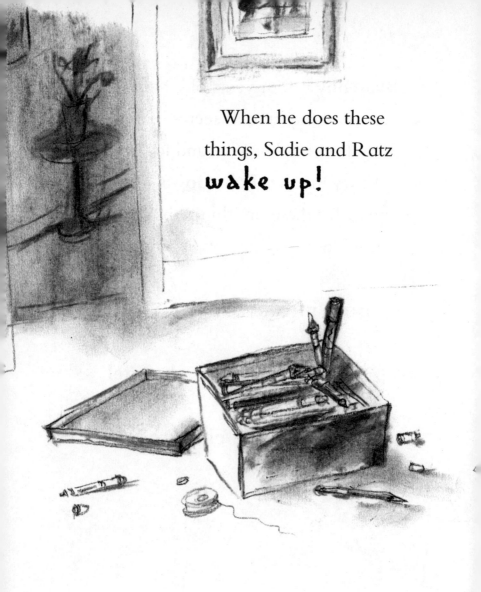

When he does these
things, Sadie and Ratz
wake up!

They jump onto Baby Boy's head, and try to rub his ears off.

Baby Boy doesn't like it. He bellows like a banshee bull. Baby Boy bellows and then I get in trouble, even though Baby Boy caused the trouble in the first place. If he didn't annoy me, Sadie and Ratz wouldn't have to rub his ears off.

Mum says I must be patient. She says, "Baby Boy is only little." She says Sadie and Ratz should do yoga. She says, "They might learn to relax."

These are yoga positions Mum thinks
Sadie and Ratz could try:

"Snowflakes
in Winter"

"Starfish"

"The Rambling River"

Sadie and Ratz invented their own positions:

"The Lion's Mane"
"The Hammerheads"
"Long Lightning Bolts"

They showed Baby Boy the Hammerheads. He screeched like a banshee bull.

Chapter Two

On Saturday, at our house, something strange happened. I was drawing pictures, and Baby Boy was wandering around. Suddenly some felt-tip was on the wall. It was a long black line on the clean white wall.

"Who did this?" asked Dad.

This is when the strange thing happened.

Normally Baby Boy would pretend he hadn't heard Dad's question. He would pretend he was a spaceman who couldn't hear a sound. Instead of owning up to drawing on the wall, he would act like he was deaf.

But this day, this strange day, Baby Boy yelled, "Sadie and Ratz did it!"

Sadie and Ratz **woke up!** They showed Baby Boy their claws.

But Baby Boy was hiding behind
Dad, safe from attack.

"Sadie and Ratz should be more
careful," said Dad, scrubbing the wall.
Baby Boy peeked out at me, and
smiled like a crazy monkey.

Later, after dinner, when Baby Boy
was playing with trucks, Sadie and
Ratz showed him their new yoga
position:

"The Shark's Teeth"

Baby Boy did the banshee bull thing.
I got sent to bed.
As usual.

That was a strange day, but things
were about to get stranger.

On Sunday morning, when milk got
on the carpet, Baby Boy told Mum,
"Sadie and Ratz did it."

That afternoon, when he skinned his knee, Baby Boy told Grandma, "Sadie and Ratz pushed me."

Even though Sadie and Ratz had not spilled milk or pushed Baby Boy,
I didn't say anything.
I just gave
Baby Boy
a cold stare.

Grandma gave Baby Boy a kiss
and a biscuit. I only got a biscuit.

I could not understand why my
brother was telling these fibs. Maybe
he wanted his ears rubbed so hard
they disappeared.

That night, when Baby Boy was in bed, Sadie and Ratz and I crept into his room. "Do you want your ears rubbed off your head?" we asked.

Baby Boy's eyes made circles. He was about to yell like a whole herd of banshee bulls. Sadie and Ratz had no choice but to **attack!**

Mum and Dad came running. I got
The Stern Talk. Baby Boy got more
kisses.

Everything was wrong.

At school on Monday,
I took my lunch to
a corner where
nobody goes.
I needed
some private
time. I ate my
sandwich and
thought.

Baby Boy was only four, but he was becoming tricky.

It was better when he was a spaceman who never heard or spoke. Sadie and Ratz liked doing bad things, but they didn't like getting in trouble for bad things they didn't do.

But everyone knew Sadie and Ratz were naughty. Everybody believed the worst when it came to Sadie and Ratz.

I ate my sandwich slowly. I wondered what Baby Boy was doing at home. I wondered what he was breaking or wrecking. I wondered what Sadie and Ratz would get the blame for today.

41

A horrible thought came into my
head. Maybe Sadie and Ratz would
have to change. Maybe the only way
to stop Baby Boy blaming Sadie and
Ratz for everything was to tame them,
and make them nice.

No! I couldn't do it. It would break
Sadie and Ratz's hearts.

43

Because they were sad, I let Sadie
and Ratz have a war with each other.
Sadie won, but it was close. They are
both good fighters.

Chapter Three

On Tuesday, my stick insect, Pin, was missing a leg. At breakfast, he had six legs. At dinner, he had five!

This was too much.

I made the noise like the banshee bull.

"Baby Boy stole Pin's leg!" I wailed.

"Don't be silly," said Dad. "It probably just fell off. Maybe Pin ate it? Insects do funny things."

"Pin did not eat his leg!" I thundered. "Baby Boy pulled it off!"

"Baby Boy is a good boy," said Mum. "He wouldn't do something as naughty as that."

I jumped up and down. I kicked the wall. "If *he* didn't do it, who did?"

From where he was hiding, in the laundry basket, Baby Boy shouted, "Sadie and Ratz!"

But even Mum
and Dad knew that
Sadie and Ratz
wouldn't hurt Pin.
Mum looked at Dad.
Dad looked at Mum.
Both of them looked
worried.

I started to cry. "Baby Boy will get
Pin out of his cage, and Pin will escape,
and Dad will step on him!"

"No, no," said Mum,
"I'm sure he wouldn't
do that!"

"Oh no!" said Dad.
"I'm sure I won't do that!"

But neither of them
looked very sure about
anything.

Something peculiar
was going on in
our house.

That night, Sadie and Ratz wanted
to rub Baby Boy's ears, nose, hair and
chin right off his head. But I knew that
would cause more strife. Baby Boy
knew it too. Baby Boy was little, but
he was crafty.

I said, "Sadie and Ratz, you must go on holiday." It was the best idea I had. If Sadie and Ratz were far away, Baby Boy couldn't get them into trouble.

Sadie wanted to go where they make movies.

Ratz wanted to go where there were pinball machines.

They waved goodbye, and set off on holiday.

The next day, I was lonely. I was sad at school. At home, I lay on my bed and drew pictures, and ate some cheese sticks. I took Pin out of his cage and let him wobble up my arm.

When Pin had had his exercise, I put
him back in his cage.
 I sighed.

I missed Sadie and Ratz already.

Suddenly Baby Boy bellowed. Mum,
Dad and I followed the sound. Baby
Boy was standing in the sitting-room,
pointing to Mum's precious
clock. It was a tiny clock.
It was a hundred years
old. It lay on the floor
in a hundred pieces.
It wasn't making its
usual ticking noise.

Mum's eyes made circles. "What happened?" she asked.

"Sadie and Ratz," said Baby Boy.

"That's not true!" I shouted. "Sadie and Ratz are on holiday!"

"I didn't do it!" said Baby Boy.
Mum and Dad looked at me, and
then at Baby Boy. Mum picked up
some bits of clock. The bits
were tiny. The biggest
bit was the clock's
round face.

The small hand was pointing to the number 2.

The big hand was pointing to the number 12.

Mum said, "The clock stopped ticking at two o'clock."

At two o'clock, Sadie and Ratz had been playing pinball, and I had been at school.

Dad wouldn't break Mum's clock, and Mum wouldn't either, and neither would Pin.

Which left only one suspect.

But Baby Boy was a good boy. At least, that's what everyone thought.

And then we guessed who had *really* been drawing on walls, spilling milk, stealing legs and breaking clocks.

We all looked down at Baby Boy's hands. Baby Boy smiled like a happy, crazy monkey.

"Oh dear," said Dad.

"Oh no," sighed Mum.

"Hooray!" I said. Because when Sadie and Ratz came home from holiday, they were going to meet two new friends.

Baby Boy said their names were

Colin and Scraps.